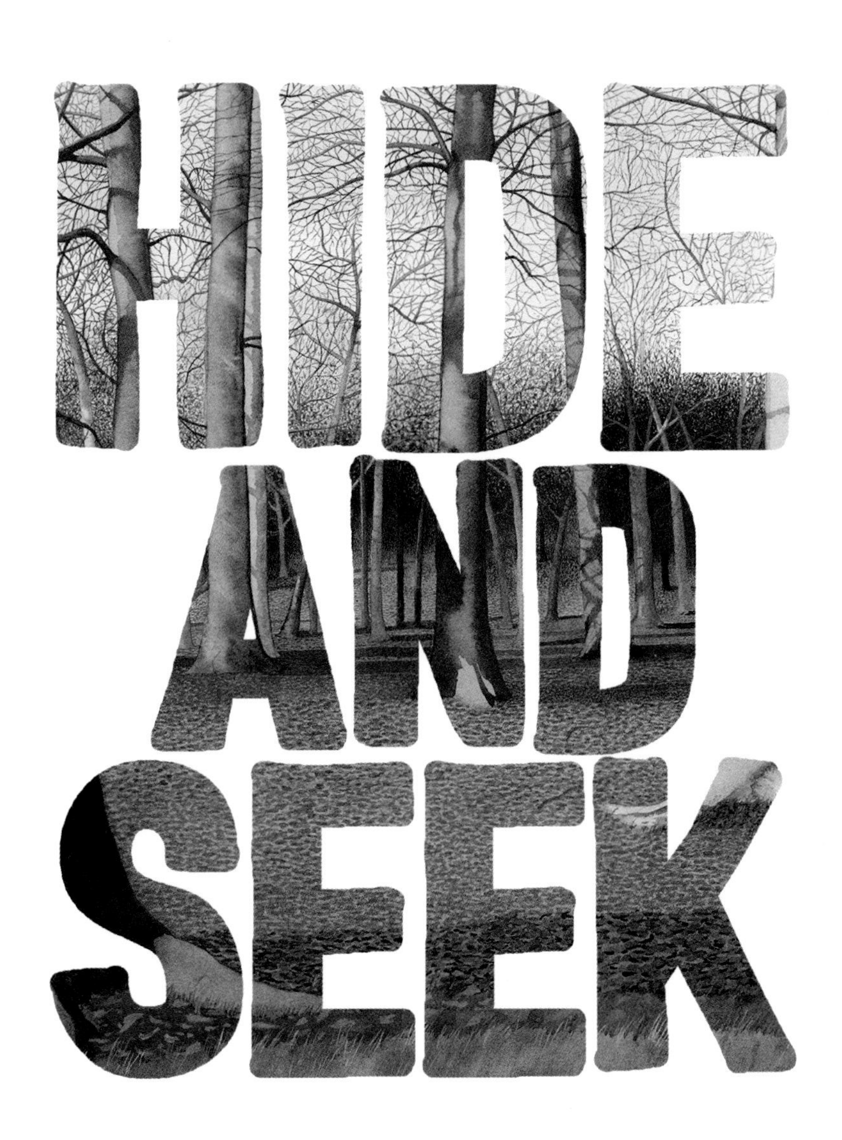
HIDE
AND
SEEK

for Hanne

Some other books by Anthony Browne

King Kong
Me and You
My Brother
My Mum
My Dad
The Shape Game
Voices in the Park
What If...?
Willy and Hugh
Willy the Wizard

DOUBLEDAY
UK | USA | Canada | Ireland | Australia
India | New Zealand | South Africa

Doubleday is part of the Penguin Random House group of companies
whose addresses can be found at global.penguinrandomhouse.com.

www.penguin.co.uk www.puffin.co.uk www.ladybird.co.uk

First published 2017
001

Printed in China
A CIP catalogue record for this book is available from the British Library

ISBN: 978-0-857-53491-0

All correspondence to:
Doubleday, Penguin Random House Children's, 80 Strand, London WC2R 0RL

Anthony Browne

DOUBLEDAY

Poppy and Cy had been sad for a few days,
ever since their dog, Goldie, had disappeared.
They sat . . .

and sat . . .
and thought about what to do.
"Shall we play something?" asked Cy.

"But what shall we play?" replied Poppy.
"What about cards?"

"Boring!" said Cy. "I want to play monsters!"

"Monsters are **stupid**," said Poppy.
"Why don't we go outside?"

"But what **shall** we play?" sighed Cy.

"**You** come up with something,"
said Poppy.

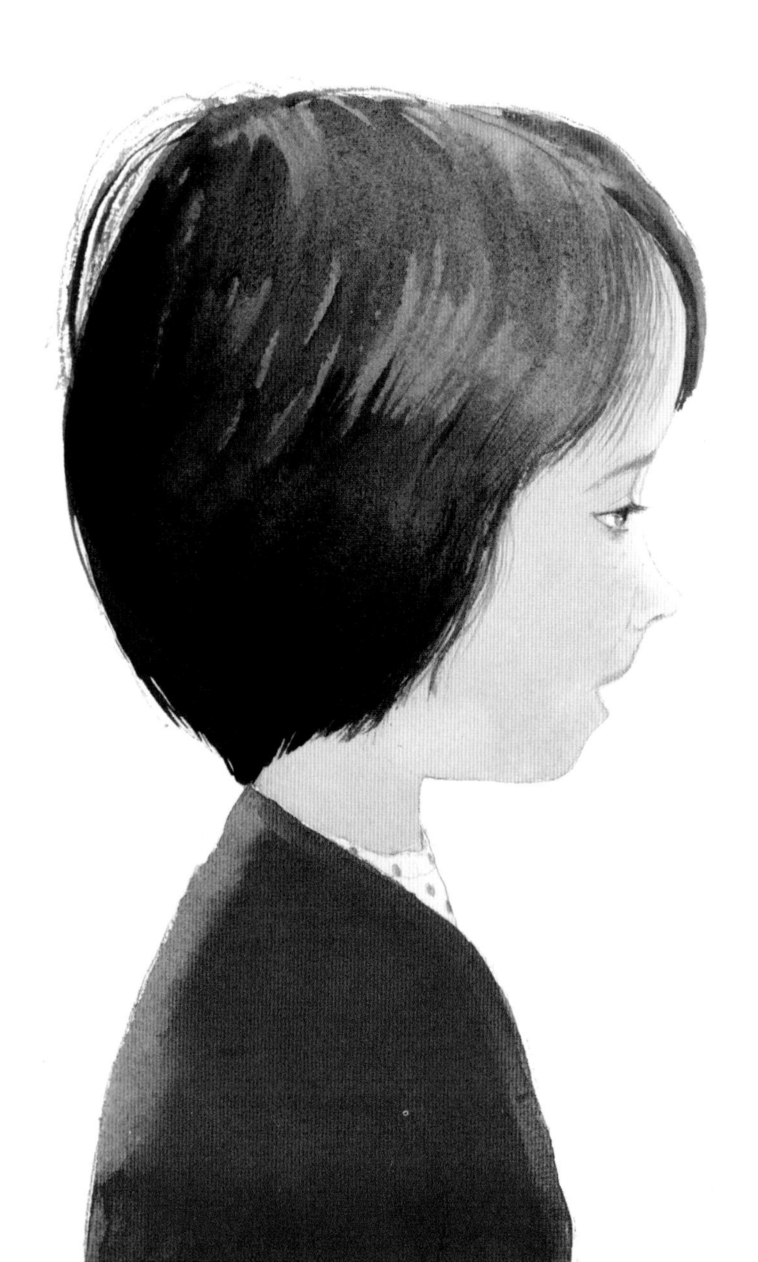

"How about hide-and-seek?" said Cy.

"Excellent," said Poppy. "Why don't you go as far into the woods as you can, and then I'll come and look for you."

Cy ran off as Poppy counted.

"One, two, three, four . . ."

". . . five, six,

seven,
eight."

Cy ran deep into the forest
and found a tangle of branches.

This is a good place, he thought.
She'll **never** find me here.

"Nine . . . ten . . . Coming – ready or not!"

Poppy finished counting and strolled into the woods.

Cy was excited – he was so well hidden!
He knew he must be quiet . . .

But he couldn't stop shaking.

Poppy thought she'd find Cy quickly
– he always chose such easy places to hide.
He's probably behind that tree . . .

But he wasn't.

Oh no, thought Cy. I think I need a wee!
Why does this always happen when I hide?
I wonder if Poppy will find me soon . . .

But Poppy was still a long way away.

He can't have gone **far,** she thought.
Perhaps he's hiding behind that pile of logs.

But he wasn't.

Will it be too hard for Poppy to find me here? thought Cy.

Where is Cy? Maybe he's behind that fallen tree . . .

He isn't.

I wish she'd come and find me, thought Cy.
I hope she hasn't gone home and left me.

He **must** be over there, thought Poppy.

He's not!

I'm getting cold now, thought Cy.
I want to go **home**.

I didn't mean for him to come this far into the woods . . .

What's that noise? I must find Cy!

What's
that
noise?
Is it
Poppy –
or a
monster?

"Found you! Both of you!"

"I was **really** worried about you!" said Poppy.

"I was a bit worried too," said Cy,
"but Goldie's back and now everything is OK!"

"Let's go home now," said Poppy.

So they all did, together.

What else is hiding in the forest? Did you see…

The armchair
The bone
The cans
The collar
The crocodile
The dogs
The duck
The ear
The elephant's trunk
The faces
The giraffe
The hat
The lead
The paw
The spear
The tap
The trumpet
The walking stick

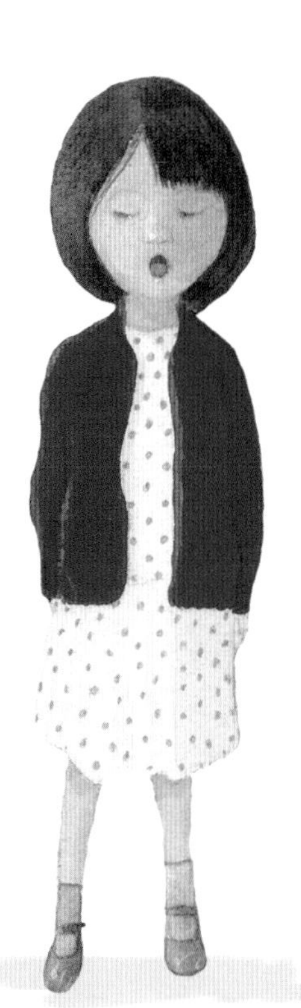

There's lots more to find . . .